Lana, The Llama Who Wants To Be A Unicorn

by

Sonica Ellis

Illustrated by Harriet Rodis

Dear Reader,

I wrote this book for *you*. I want you to know that you are loved and wonderfully made, so don't let anyone tell you otherwise.

You don't need to look like anyone but yourself to be beautiful.
And I will tell you a secret ... Just like a unicorn, *you have magic within you!*

I hope you enjoy this book and don't forget you are awesome.

Yours Truly,

Sonica Ellis

Copyright (C) 2019
ISBN: 978-0-578-49718-1

DEDICATION:

This book is dedicated to you...*yes you!*

Release your inner magic!

Lana the Llama would visit the pond by the bridge everyday
to watch the unicorns as they soared happily through the sky,
leaving a sparkling trail of magic behind them.

Although she watched, Lana never spoke to them, worried that because she was different they would not like her.

"I'm going to be a unicorn when I grow up.
I'm going to be beautiful, enchanting and magical
just like the other unicorns."

Each day Lana would tell her family that
she was going to be a unicorn when she grew up.

Lana would even ask her friends the same question *every day!*
"Do you know what I am going to be when I grow up?"

She would ask it so often the other animals would roll their eyes and reply
"Yes Lana, **we know**... you are going to be a Unicorn when you grow up."

Lana would say this so often that Mama and Papa Llama
decided they needed to have a talk with her
and explain that she *can't* be a unicorn
when she grows up.

"Lana sweetheart, you are a *llama*
and you are special and beautiful
just the way you are."

"No!

I *am* going to be a unicorn
when I grow up!

You just wait and see!"

Later that night...

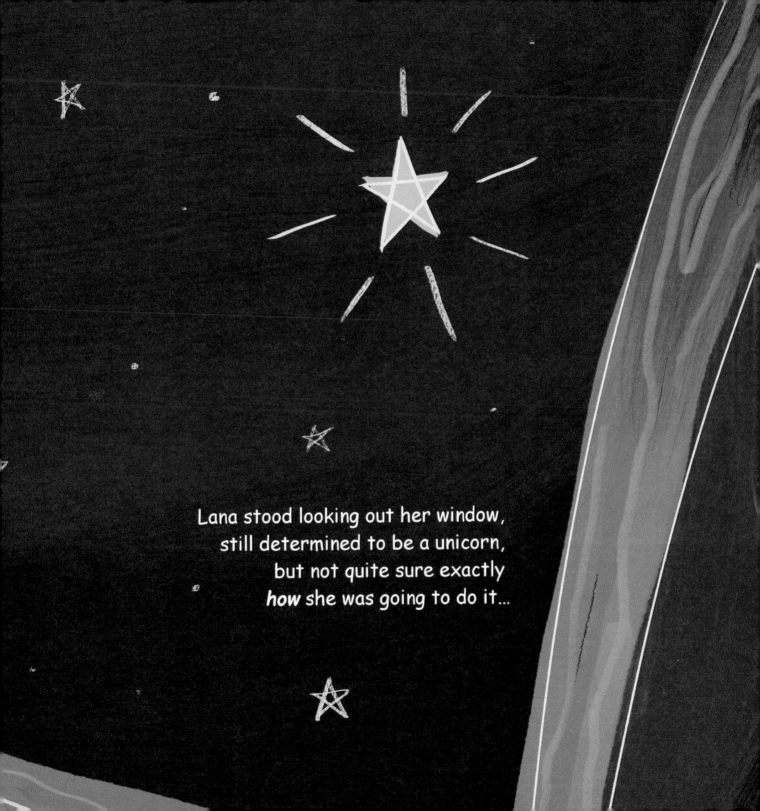

Lana stood looking out her window,
still determined to be a unicorn,
but not quite sure exactly
how she was going to do it...

Until one day Lana had a wonderful idea!

Lana gathered a party hat, construction paper, scissors, tape, and glitter from Mama Llama's craft kit...

...and raced up the stairs!

When she was finished Lana ran down the stairs, out the door,
and straight to the pond
where the unicorns could always be found playing.

Lana walked excitedly to where a pair of unicorns was playing
and introduced herself.
Because she now had a horn and wings herself,
Lana was feeling as confident as could be.

"My name is Lana" she said, "what is your name?"
"I am Ellie" replied the unicorn, "Nice to meet you!"

Lana and Ellie played throughout the day until it was time to go home.
"It is almost dinner time" said Lana, "and I should be going now."
"OK" said Ellie smiling, "I will walk you home."

When they arrived Ellie told Lana what a wonderful time she had playing together. "I had a great time playing with you Lana. Maybe tomorrow you can come back as the *real* you?"

Lana was surprised. "You knew I was not a *real* unicorn?" she asked a bit embarrassed.

"I did," replied Ellie, "but I want you to know that you don't need a horn and wings to be special.

There is magic inside you just the way you are!"

As Lana hugged Ellie goodbye she realized that Mama and Papa Llama were right all along.

Everyone is special and beautiful just the way they are.

Made in the USA
Middletown, DE
12 August 2020